Merlin

The Magical Puppy

Annual 2003

KEITH LITTLER

Contents

Published by Carlton Books Ltd 2002

20 Mortimer Street
London W1T 3JW

Text and design Copyright © 2002 Carlton Book s Ltd

Photographs Copyright © 2002 The Little Entertainment Company/Entertainment Rights PLC.

TM © 2002 LEC/Entertaiment Rights PLC. All rights reserved.

ISBN 1 84222 629 0.

A CIP catalogue for this book is available from the British Library.

Project Editor: Lesley Levene
Art Director: Clare Baggaley
Design: Anita Ruddell
Production: Lisa French

CARLTON
BOOKS

Ten Things to Know about Merlin

1 Merlin is a black Labrador puppy.

2 Merlin is looked after by Ernie, the Harbour Master.

3 Merlin has his own kennel right next to Ernie's hut at Sandybay Harbour.

4 Merlin's favourite food is sausages.

5 Merlin's favourite toy is his orange ball.

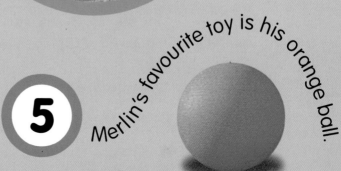

6 Merlin's best friends are Kizzie, Reg the Hedge (short for hedgehog) and Charlotte.

7 Merlin loves digging holes. He gets into trouble when he digs them in people's gardens.

8 Merlin loves having a bath.

9 Merlin hates cats – especially Oscar the cat.

10 Merlin loves to sleep in front of a warm fire.

Meet the Characters from

Mr Pickles

Miss Parkway

Albert

Reg

Kizzie

Merlin

Sandybay Harbour

Ernie

Mr Crabtree

Mrs Crabtree

Gull

Charlotte

Oscar

Miss Parkway

Miss Parkway is a teacher at a nearby school. She looks after Kizzie and likes everything to be "just so".

Oscar

Oscar has lived in Sandybay for a long time. Most days he takes a walk along the harbour, watching the fishermen and hoping to be given a fish or two! He also likes to torment Merlin.

Kizzie

Kizzie is Merlin's best friend and she lives with Miss Parkway. She likes to look as pretty as possible and loves her sparkly blue collar.

Ernie, the Harbour Master

Ernie looks after Merlin. It is his job to make sure that everything runs smoothly in Sandybay Harbour.

Mr Pickles

Mr Pickles used to be the captain of a fishing boat. He is retired now but still loves fishing and telling stories about his time at sea.

Charlotte

Charlotte often comes to stay with her uncle and aunt, who own the shop in Sandybay Harbour. She loves to play with Merlin and Kizzie.

Mr and Mrs Crabtree

Mr and Mrs Crabtree own the shop in Sandybay Harbour. It is the main place to go for news and gossip.

Gull

Gull loves to fly to Sandybay Harbour, looking for fish. His favourite spot to stop and rest is the barrel next to Merlin's kennel.

Albert

Albert owns a magic shop and is Ernie's great friend.

Reg the Hedge

Reg the Hedge lives in a garden in Sandybay. He does everything very slowly, including his favourite pastime: walking about!

Merlin and the Lost Bone

Merlin was looking for his bone. He remembered that he had buried it in a garden, but he couldn't remember which one. He decided to dig a hole in all of the gardens, but he still couldn't find his lost bone.

Merlin was so busy digging that he didn't see Miss Parkway looking at him from her kitchen door. She was not very happy.

"Hey!" Miss Parkway called loudly, and Merlin nearly jumped out of his skin. "What are you doing? Look at my garden!"

The garden was a bit of a mess. Merlin decided that now might be a good time to disappear, especially as Miss Parkway was about to throw her slipper at him.

The people of Sandybay Harbour were not happy to find this little puppy digging up their flower beds and lovely lawns. They all complained to Ernie, the Harbour Master. "You really have to do something about your puppy," they said.

Ernie decided to drive to Newby to buy Merlin a collar and a lead. He parked his car outside Albert's Magic Shop.

"Hello, Ernie," Albert called. "How are things in Sandybay Harbour?"

Ernie told his friend all about the complaints he had received because of Merlin and his habit of digging up gardens.

"I may have just the thing," Albert said. "It will save you a trip to the pet shop." Albert showed Ernie a smart red collar with a golden buckle. "It's very old," Albert explained, "and I hear it is magic."

Ernie thought the collar looked wonderful. "I'll take it," he said.

13

Merlin was pleased with his new collar and he felt very grown up walking about the harbour with it around his neck. It even had a little silver disc with his name on it.

"I wonder if it really is magic," he thought. "If it is, then I could use it to find my lost bone." He decided to try chasing his tail, which is something all puppies love to do. "Find my lost bone now!" he barked.

Nothing much happened, except that Merlin felt a bit dizzy.

"This collar is not magic at all," he sighed. "I wish I could find my lost bone."

Well, as soon as Merlin said the magic word, "wish", his collar began to flash and sparkle. Suddenly he was back in the garden where the lady with the flying slipper lived.

"Wow!" Merlin barked. "My magic collar worked."

But Merlin couldn't dig for his lost bone because Miss Parkway was in her greenhouse and she would be sure to see him. He decided to use his magic collar again, only this time he would make himself invisible.

Merlin chased his tail. "She'll never see me now and I can dig as much as I like," he barked. But because he had not said the magic word, "wish", his collar did not work and he was not invisible. Merlin started digging.

"Hey, you!" Miss Parkway called. "What do you think you are doing?"

Merlin was surprised. "I'm supposed to be invisible," he whined. "My magic collar didn't work!"

Merlin knew that if Miss Parkway caught him digging again, he would be in trouble with Ernie. "Oh, I wish I was invisible," he barked.

As soon as Merlin said the magic word, "wish", his collar flashed and sparkled. Miss Parkway stopped suddenly and scratched her head. "How strange," she said. "He seems to have disappeared."

Merlin was enjoying being invisible. He walked along the harbour and saw Oscar about to eat a large juicy fish. This was his chance to get back at Oscar for all the times the cat had been mean to him. He sneaked up and quickly grabbed the fish.

Oscar was amazed. His fish seemed to be floating all by itself. It went this way and that. Merlin was laughing very hard…which isn't easy when your mouth is full of fish!

But then Merlin heard Ernie calling him. "Merlin! Your dinner is ready!" Merlin ran back to his kennel. "I'm here," he barked. But Ernie couldn't see him because he was still invisible.

"Oh, well," Ernie said. "He must be out playing. I'll save these sausages for later."

"But I'm here!" Merlin barked.

Oh dear. Poor Merlin had lost his bone and missed his dinner.

"I wish people could see me again!" he whined, and as soon as Merlin said the magic word, "wish", his collar flashed and sparkled and he reappeared.

"Ah, Merlin, there you are," Ernie said. "I've got some sausages for you."

Merlin was very happy. "Hmmmm, lovely hot sausages beat a buried bone any day."

Hunt the Bone

Can you help find Merlin's missing bones?

Merlin has buried six bones in Miss Parkway's garden. He has asked Kizzie and Reg the Hedge to help him look for them. See if you can find them first.

19

Looking after a Puppy of Your Own

A puppy is not a toy to be left in the cupboard if you grow bored with it. A puppy is part of the family and, just like a child, it will grow up. Here is Merlin's guide to looking after your own puppy.

We like exercise

Walks are fantastic. They give us a chance to see what's happening and have a good sniff about. I think if a puppy had a favourite word it would be "walkies". We can also get a lot of exercise from playing. My favourite game is chasing my orange ball. I love it when Ernie or Charlotte throws it for me.

We love food

A good diet is very important for any pet. The right food makes us fit and healthy. The trouble is that we puppies like everything, and that can be a problem. Sweets and chocolates are not good for us. A vet will tell you the treats we can eat without making us fat or poorly. Our favourite drink is water…and lots of it!

We like being with people

Just like anyone else, we puppies get sad if we are left alone for too long. We want to see what is going on and we enjoy being with people. We really love it when you talk to us and play with us. We like to go everywhere and anywhere with you, but be careful not to leave us alone in houses for too long, or in cars when it's hot, as this can be very dangerous for a dog.

We like to be clean

Every now and again we get quite dirty from running about outside. I particularly like digging and running through puddles! It is really nice to be given a bath and to have my fur combed.

We like to learn

Puppies can be naughty sometimes. Just like children, we need to be told what to do and how to do it. We call that training. Good training means that we don't mind walking on a lead, we remember to go outside for the toilet and we know not to jump all over the furniture and chew visitors' shoes!

Merlin and the Gold Medal

Everyone in Sandybay was talking about the Winter Olympics. Merlin was sure he could win a gold medal. He was good at running, good at jumping and especially good at chasing his tail.

He decided to use his magic collar. He chased his tail round and round and barked, "I want to win a gold medal now!" But nothing happened.

Merlin had forgotten how his magic collar worked again. "Oh, I wish I could win a gold medal," he sighed. As soon as he said the magic word, "wish", his collar began to flash and sparkle.

Suddenly Merlin was standing beneath snow-topped mountains and Mr Crabtree was there with a clipboard.

"Wow," Merlin barked. "My magic collar did work."

Mr Crabtree checked his watch, then looked up. "Are you ready, Merlin?"

Reg the Hedge was sitting in a special sledge called a bobsleigh. Mr Crabtree explained that Merlin had to give the sledge a big push and then jump on the back.

"Ready," Merlin barked.

A horn blew and Merlin pushed the sledge as hard as he could. In fact, he pushed it too hard and it shot off down the hill without him.

"Help!" Reg the Hedge called.

The sledge went down the course, getting quicker and quicker, with Merlin sliding right behind it.

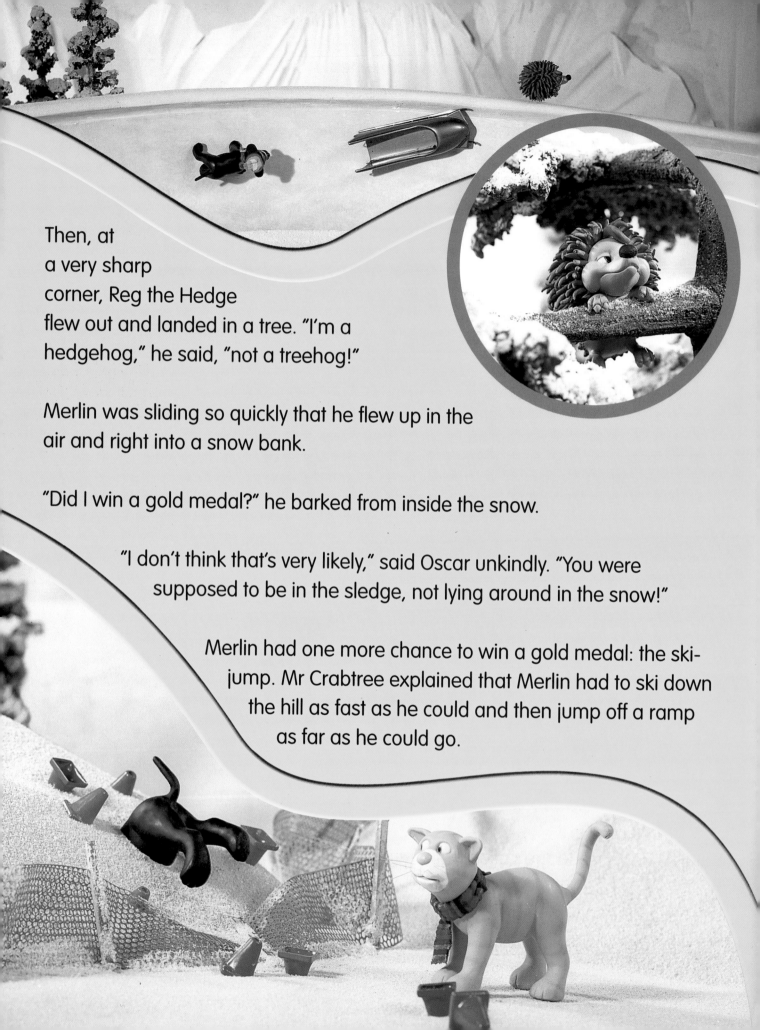

Then, at
a very sharp
corner, Reg the Hedge
flew out and landed in a tree. "I'm a
hedgehog," he said, "not a treehog!"

Merlin was sliding so quickly that he flew up in the
air and right into a snow bank.

"Did I win a gold medal?" he barked from inside the snow.

"I don't think that's very likely," said Oscar unkindly. "You were
supposed to be in the sledge, not lying around in the snow!"

Merlin had one more chance to win a gold medal: the ski-
jump. Mr Crabtree explained that Merlin had to ski down
the hill as fast as he could and then jump off a ramp
as far as he could go.

Merlin waited for the starter horn to blow, then off he went. He zoomed down the hill, going quicker and quicker, and then he jumped. But he had forgotten to fasten his skis on properly and they flew off. Poor Merlin landed in a pile of snow yet again.

"Great news," Mr Crabtree cried. "You've won the gold medal and broken the world distance record!"

"Oh, good," Merlin mumbled from inside the snow. "But I wish I could go home."

As soon as Merlin said the magic word, "wish", his collar flashed and sparkled and he appeared safely back in front of his kennel. "Phew," he barked. "I made it."

Merlin had enjoyed being in the ice and snow, but he now realized just how difficult all of the events could be. In future he thought he might stick to watching the Winter Olympics on the television.

Merlin's Olympic Race Game

Start

Be like Merlin and try to win a gold medal. Join the race with a friend and see who gets to the finishing line first. You'll need a dice and two counters. Throw the dice and whoever gets the highest number starts. Then just move your counter along the course, following the instructions as you go. Good luck!

9 You have hit a cone – go back two squares

8 You are a champion skier – zoom forward three squares

10 You have got lost – go back four squares

11

12 You have found a shor cut – have another go

1

2 You have lost your hat – go back to the beginning

3 The wind is behind you – go forward two squares

4

5

6

7

13

14 You have fallen into a snow bank – go back to square 5

15

Finish

Congratulations – you are now a gold medallist!

27

Working Dogs

Merlin is a pet, but did you know that many dogs work for a living? Here are a few dogs that do very important jobs.

Guide dogs

Guide dogs are usually Golden Labradors but sometimes other breeds of dog are used, such as German Shepherds or Black Labradors like Merlin. Carefully trained to guide blind people, they have a close relationship with their owners and become very good friends with them.

Mountain rescue dogs

Mountain rescue dogs are usually St Bernards. Large and strong, they are capable of walking up and down mountains. They are also intelligent and gentle, so they are the perfect dog for finding people who are stuck or injured on a mountain.

Police dogs

Police dogs are usually Alsatians, which are also called German Shepherds. These are very strong and fast dogs. They are trained to do many jobs, including crowd control and helping the police in their fight against smugglers and burglars.

Sheep dogs

Sheep dogs are usually Border Collies. They are very clever at rounding up sheep and making a whole flock go in the direction the farmer wants them to. The farmer uses a series of whistles and signals to tell the dog what to do and which direction to go in.

Sled dogs

In places where there is a lot of snow, people get around on sledges (known as sleds in America). These are pulled by packs of very strong dogs belonging to a breed called Husky. As you can imagine, they have thick fur to keep them warm in the cold weather.

Merlin and the Maze

Merlin needs to get through the maze to meet Kizzie and Oscar. Can you help him to find his way?

Start

Finish

Merlin – Secret Agent

Ernie and Merlin were at home, enjoying a peaceful evening. Ernie was reading one of his favourite books about secret agents. Merlin thought the story was very exciting.

When Ernie went to the kitchen to make a cup of tea, Merlin decided to try his magic collar. He chased his tail round and round. "Make me a secret agent," he barked.

But nothing happened, except that he nearly tripped over the carpet!

"Oh, I can never remember how this collar works," he whined. "I wish I could be a secret agent."

As soon as Merlin said the magic word, "wish", his collar flashed and sparkled.

Suddenly Merlin was standing in the middle of nowhere and wondering if his collar had broken. "Calling Agent Merlin," said a voice. "Calling Agent Merlin."

Merlin looked down and realized that the voice was coming from his secret-agent watch radio. "Great!" he barked. "My magic collar worked. I am a secret agent and I have a secret gadget. All good agents have secret gadgets."

The watch radio explained that the evil Dr Whiskers had kidnapped Kizzie and that Agent Reg the Hedge would soon be along to help Merlin rescue her. He didn't have to wait long. In seconds, Agent Reg had appeared on a ski-mobile.

"I like being a secret agent," Merlin barked. "This is exciting. Can I drive?"

Agent Merlin and Agent Reg searched everywhere for Kizzie but they couldn't find her. Merlin was so busy looking around that he didn't see a large mountain right in front of them.

"Look out!" Agent Reg called.

But it was too late. With a loud bang, the ski mobile crashed through the side of the mountain.

What a surprise! They had accidentally driven in through the secret entrance to Dr Whisker's hideaway.

"Oh, Merlin!" Kizzie barked. "I knew you would come and rescue me."

Dr Whiskers was not so happy. The crash had knocked him into a cupboard and everything inside had fallen on to his head.

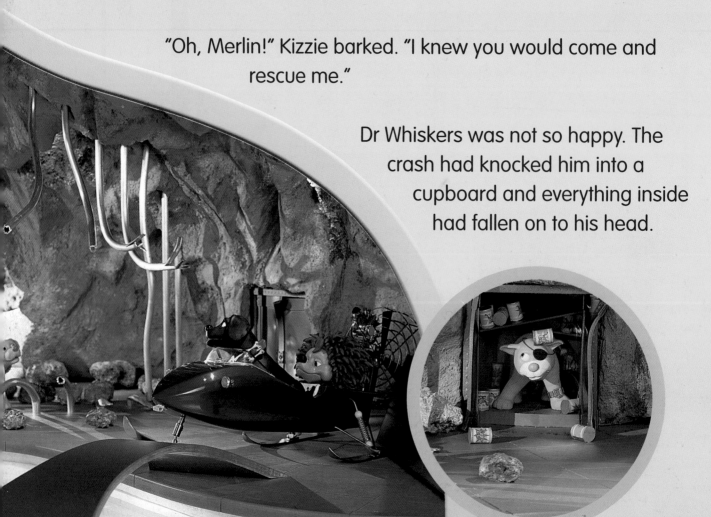

Agent Merlin pointed his secret-agent gadget at Dr Whiskers. "Stay right there," he barked bravely, "or I will stun you with my special-agent stun ray."

"Actually, it's a watch radio," Agent Reg said.

"Ha! I have you now," Dr Whiskers purred. "I am going to get you with my freeze ray."

Dr Whiskers fired at Merlin, who was frozen solid.

"And now you too, Spiky," the evil Dr Whiskers said to Agent Reg.

But he missed and the ray bounced towards Kizzie. Just in time, she managed to deflect it with her shiny collar so that it hit Dr Whiskers instead. Now he was frozen too, just like Merlin.

"Well done, Kizzie," Agent Reg said. "You saved us."

Merlin wasn't very happy, though. "I wanted to save you," he barked through his frozen teeth. "I wish I'd never wanted to be a secret agent."

As soon as Merlin said the magic word, "wish", his collar flashed and sparkled and he was safely back in front of the warm fire in Ernie's living room.

Ernie returned from the kitchen. "Do you know what, Merlin? There's a good film on television tonight about secret agents. Would you like to watch it?"

"No thanks," Merlin barked. "I think I've had enough of secret agents for one day, thank you."

Merlin's Favourite Colours

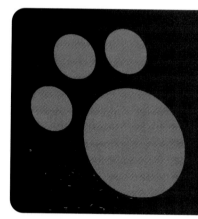

Black
I like black, the colour of
my coat,
It's soft and shiny and
perfect to stroke.

Brown
Sausages are brown and
tasty and yummy,
The best place for a sausage
is inside my tummy.

Green
Green is the colour of
grass and trees,
Where puppies can play
and do as they please.

Orange

Oscar is orange and
   I think he's fat,
He gets on my nerves, that
   tatty old cat.

Blue

Ernie's truck is big and blue,
With plenty of room in the
   front for two.

Yellow

Kizzie is yellow and my very
   best friend,
We like to play, 'til the day's at
   an end.

Red

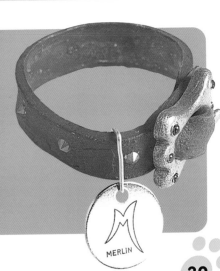

My collar is red and makes
   wishes come true,
So I'll wish for a friend who
   looks just like you.

Guiding Stars

Merlin is a popular puppy, with lots of friends in Sandybay Harbour. Recently he's met some other very special pups: Penny, Prince, Pippa, Paddy and Peds. They are training to be guide dogs. Like Merlin, they have lots of adventures. So say hello to the Pups gang and let's find out more about the fantastic world of guide dogs…

A guide dog puppy's life

You've probably seen guide dogs with their owners walking confidently along the street. Well, we'll let you into a secret… Before they grow up into clever, mature guide dogs, they are as cute, cuddly and daft as all other puppies. After a year with their puppy walkers, the young trainees move on to special centres where a trainer teaches them how to deal with traffic, to walk in a straight line and to stop when they come to a kerb. Then they are ready to meet the blind person who will become their new owner and a very special partnership begins.

> Even super-cool guide dog pups like me start off as tiny little bundles of fur. We don't do much at this stage except sleep, squeak and feed!

Penny looks sleek and cool at all times.

> When we're about six weeks old, we go to live with special people called puppy walkers. They teach us all sorts of things, like how to "sit" and "stay" when we're told to.

The leader of the gang, **Peds** is a very sensible puppy.

We need to get used to busy streets, crowded shopping centres, buses, trains and anywhere else our blind owners may take us to when we grow up.

When we're not hard at work, learning how to be guide dogs, we have fun and play like any other puppies.

Pippa is always up to mischief with her puppy pranks.

Paddy's loud bark can be heard for miles!

We have regular feeding times – my favourite part of the day.

Only one thing stops **Prince**'s tail from wagging – his tummy rumbling!

Join our club

Why not join the Pups Club? You'll receive the super-cool Pups magazine four times a year, plus a choice of two great membership gifts: either a cute, cuddly pocket-sized toy pup or a Pups pack containing all sorts of goodies.

Want to find out more? We're offering all Merlin fans a free Pups magazine, packed full of cartoons, competitions and brilliant stuff about guide dogs.

Just call 0118 983 8364 or e-mail pups@gdba.org.uk (Please remember to ask permission first from the person who pays the phone bill.) Offer closes 31st December 2003.

Free Pups magazine

Merlin and the Summer Fair

Merlin was hanging around outside his kennel one day feeling very bored.

"I've played with my favourite orange ball," he sighed, "I've played with my toy boat and I've buried a bone in Miss Parkway's garden. Now I have nothing left to do."

Merlin's best friend Kizzie had an idea. "There is a fair in a field behind the houses," she barked. "Why don't we go and play there?"

The fair was full of brightly coloured rides and attractions. "Wow, I've never been to a fair before," Merlin barked happily. He was so excited he didn't know where to start.

"Why don't you try bowling?" said Reg the Hedge. "You have to roll the ball and try to knock over the pins."

Merlin took aim and carefully rolled the ball towards the pins. There was a loud bang as they all fell down.

"Well done, Merlin," said Kizzie and Reg.

"That was great," Merlin barked. "What shall we do now?"

"You could always try the roundabout," squawked Gull.

On the roundabout there were seats in a green racing car, a yellow rocket, a red boat and a blue car. "Which one shall we go in?" Merlin barked.

"Let's go in the red boat," Kizzie barked.

Merlin and Kizzie got into the boat and the roundabout started going round and round.

Kizzie soon jumped off, but Merlin was having great fun. Then, all of a sudden, a gust of wind blew a newspaper right into his face. "I can't see," he barked. "Help! I'm getting dizzy!"

It seemed like ages before the roundabout finally stopped. Poor Merlin was very wobbly on his feet when he got off. "Oh dear, I think that's quite enough excitement for one day," he barked. "I'm ready to go home now."

Spot the Difference

Look carefully at the pictures on this page and the one opposite. Merlin has made five changes on each picture. See if you can spot them. The answers are upside down at the bottom of this page.

On this page: Kizzie's gone cross-eyed; Charlotte is holding a cupcake; the heart on Kizzie's collar is gold; a cupcake has gone missing from the picnic blanket; a brick has turned blue.

Merlin and the Ghost

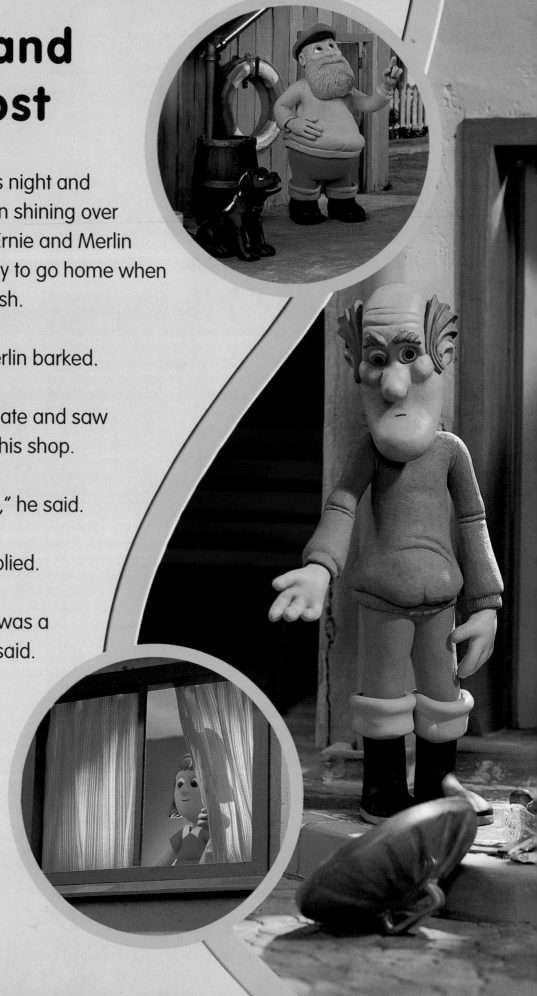

It was a dark winter's night and there was a full moon shining over Sandybay Harbour. Ernie and Merlin were just about ready to go home when there was a loud crash.

"What was that?" Merlin barked.

They went to investigate and saw Mr Crabtree outside his shop.

"I heard a loud noise," he said.

"So did we," Ernie replied.

"Charlotte thought it was a ghost," Mr Crabtree said. "She nearly jumped out of her skin."

Merlin looked up at Charlotte's window. "Don't worry," he barked. "I'll protect you."

In fact, the noise was not a ghost but Oscar looking through the dustbins for scraps of food. Merlin was disappointed. He thought it would be fun to meet a ghost. He decided to go back to his kennel and use his magic collar.

But, as usual, Merlin could not remember how his collar worked. He tried chasing his tail and barking very loudly, "I want to meet a ghost now!" But nothing happened. "Oh, I wish I could meet a ghost," he sighed.

As soon as he said the magic word, "wish", his collar flashed and sparkled.

Suddenly Merlin was transported into the back of Ernie's truck in the middle of the countryside.

Merlin was puzzled. "Did my collar work? Where's the ghost?"

He was beginning to wonder if his collar was broken when the car coughed and spluttered and then stopped.

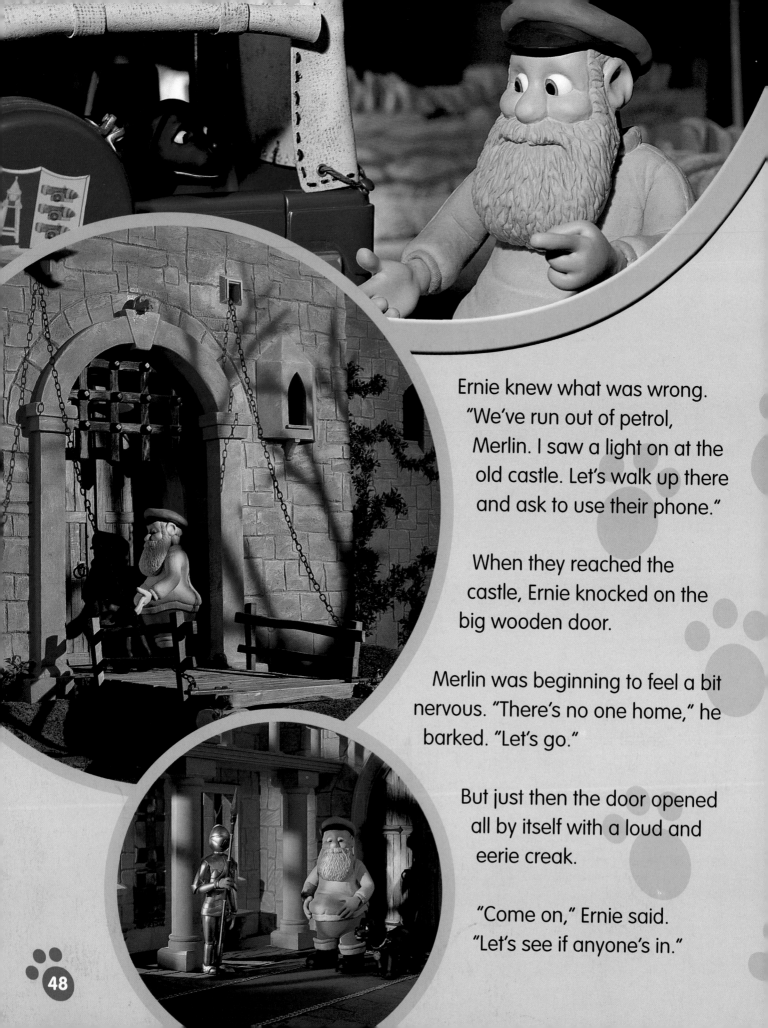

Ernie knew what was wrong. "We've run out of petrol, Merlin. I saw a light on at the old castle. Let's walk up there and ask to use their phone."

When they reached the castle, Ernie knocked on the big wooden door.

Merlin was beginning to feel a bit nervous. "There's no one home," he barked. "Let's go."

But just then the door opened all by itself with a loud and eerie creak.

"Come on," Ernie said. "Let's see if anyone's in."

They walked into the hallway and there, standing to attention, was an old suit of armour. Without any warning, the suit of armour rattled and dropped its spear on to the floor right in front of Merlin.

"Oh, no! It's a ghost!" Merlin shrieked, and he ran off to hide.

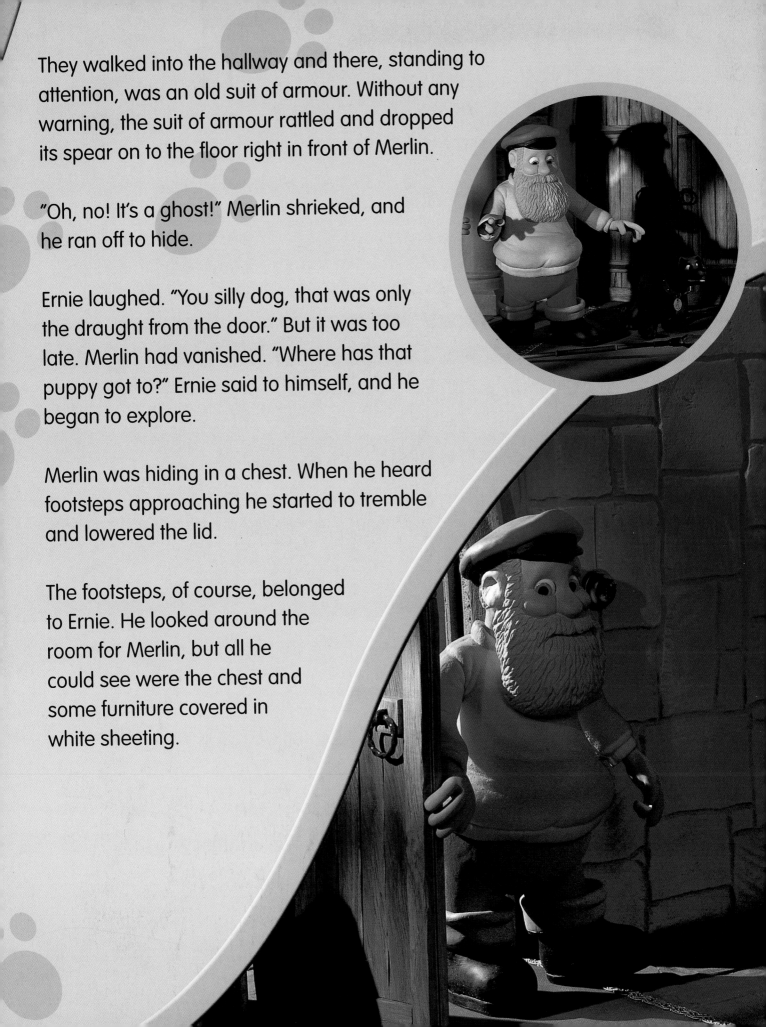

Ernie laughed. "You silly dog, that was only the draught from the door." But it was too late. Merlin had vanished. "Where has that puppy got to?" Ernie said to himself, and he began to explore.

Merlin was hiding in a chest. When he heard footsteps approaching he started to tremble and lowered the lid.

The footsteps, of course, belonged to Ernie. He looked around the room for Merlin, but all he could see were the chest and some furniture covered in white sheeting.

A sudden draught from the open door blew one of the sheets over Ernie's head. He spun round and round. When Merlin peeked out from the chest all he could see was a white spinning sheet.

"It's the ghost! I'm going to have to be brave!"

Merlin leapt from the chest and jumped on the "ghost". They rolled around the floor, puffing and panting. The "ghost" had hold of Merlin's tail and Merlin had his teeth firmly round something that felt like a hat.

Suddenly the light was switched on. It was Mr Pickles. "Whatever is happening?"

In the light, Merlin could see that it was Ernie he had jumped on. "I thought you were a ghost," he barked.

Ernie laughed. "And I thought you were a ghost!"

But Mr Pickles was not laughing. "Look at the mess," he said angrily. He was keeping an eye on the castle for the owners while they were on holiday. He had come back because he realized he had forgotten to lock the front door.

Merlin decided that he didn't want to meet a ghost any more. "I wish I was back home," he whined.

As soon as he said the magic word, "wish", his collar flashed and sparkled. Suddenly he was standing outside his kennel.

"Phew," he sighed. "I made it."

Ernie appeared, carrying a video. "Mr Crabtree said we could borrow this. It's called 'The Haunted Castle'. Shall we go home and watch it?"

"Oh, I'm not sure," Merlin barked. "I think I've had enough of ghosts for one day, thank you."

Wishes and Sausages

Playing with a friend, see if you can wish your way to the end of the game first. You'll need a dice and two counters. Throw the dice and whoever gets the highest number starts. Just work your way along the course, moving your counter up and down depending on where you land. A wish square will take you flying up, but watch out – if you land on a square at the top of a string of sausages, you'll have to come slithering down!

Hoorah! Wish your way up!

Hoorah! Wish your way up!

21 22
20 19
11 12
10 9
1 2

Start

52

23

24

25 Oh no!
Down you
go!

Finish

MERLIN

Oh no!
Down you
go!
18

17

16

13

14

Hoorah!
Wish your
way up!

8

7 Oh no!
Down you
go!

6

3

4

5

Captain Merlin

Merlin had been on the harbour front, listening to the fishermen telling stories about their days at sea. He thought it would be great to be captain of his very own fishing boat, so he decided to try his magic collar.

He chased his tail round and round. "Make me captain of my own boat," he barked. But nothing happened.

Merlin was about to give up. "Oh, I wish I could be captain of my own boat," he sighed.

As soon as Merlin said the magic word, "wish", his collar flashed and sparkled.

Suddenly Merlin was standing on the deck of the Salty Sea Dog. "Wow, my magic collar did work. I am captain of my own boat."

54

Captain Merlin turned to Ernie. "Set a course for the Island of Sausages," he barked.

"Aye, aye, sir," Ernie said, and saluted.

At the front of the boat Captain Merlin found Mr Pickles. "Do we have any food on board?" Captain Merlin asked.

"No, sir. We have to catch it. There are plenty of fish in the sea."

"Fish!" Captain Merlin did not like that. "Fish is cat food," he barked, "and I hate cats!"

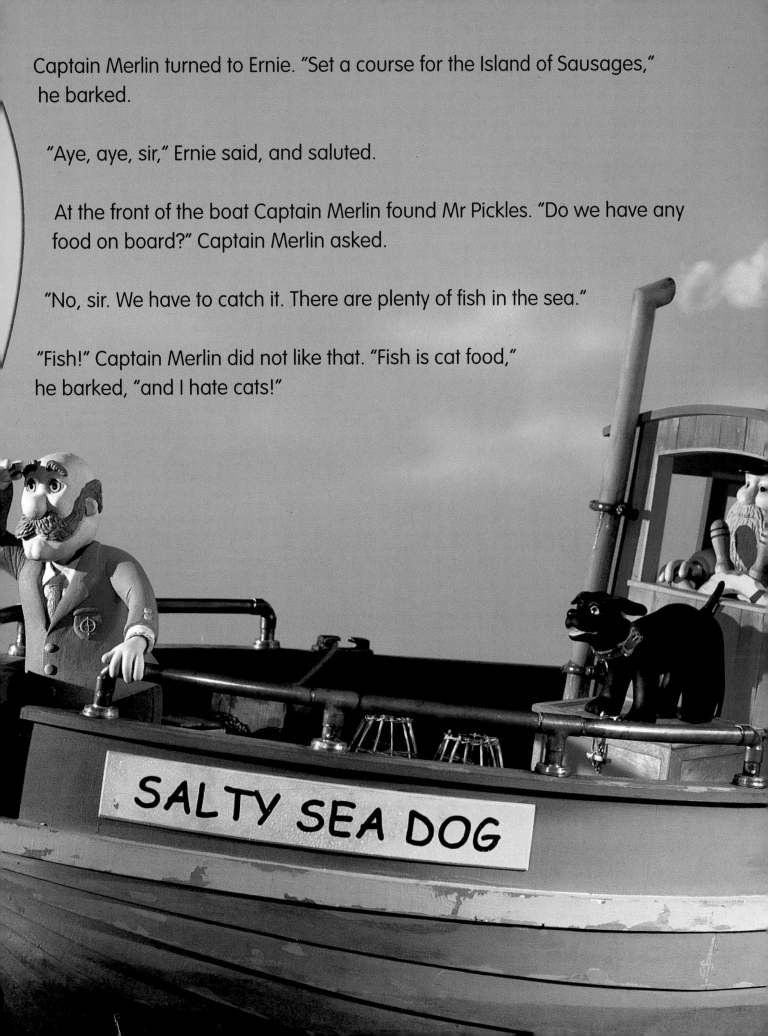

SALTY SEA DOG

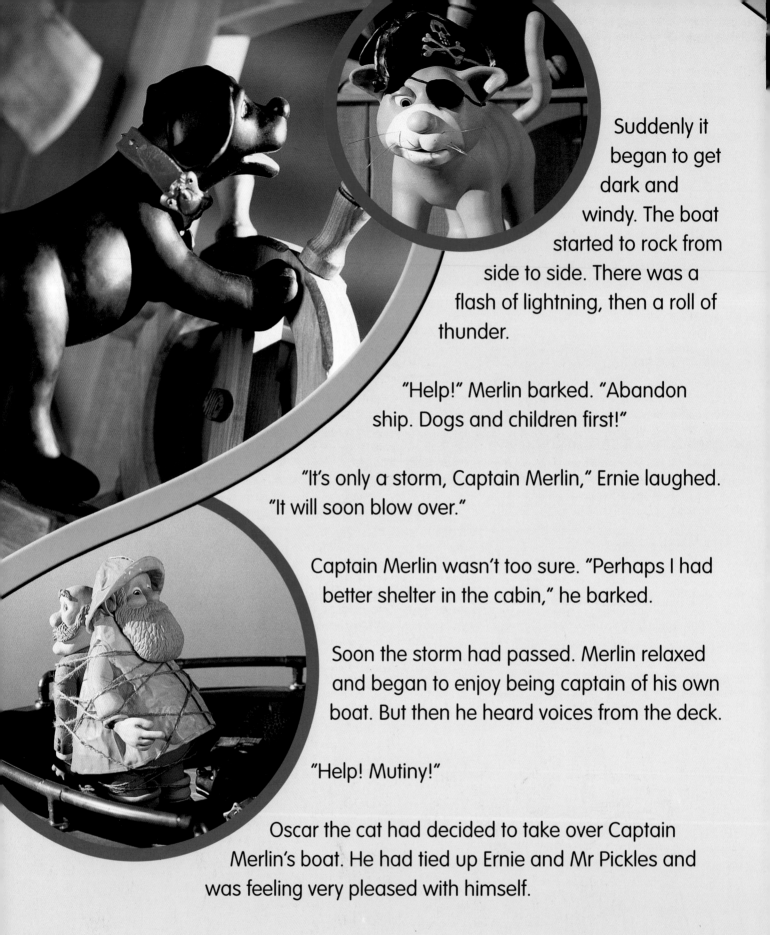

Suddenly it began to get dark and windy. The boat started to rock from side to side. There was a flash of lightning, then a roll of thunder.

"Help!" Merlin barked. "Abandon ship. Dogs and children first!"

"It's only a storm, Captain Merlin," Ernie laughed. "It will soon blow over."

Captain Merlin wasn't too sure. "Perhaps I had better shelter in the cabin," he barked.

Soon the storm had passed. Merlin relaxed and began to enjoy being captain of his own boat. But then he heard voices from the deck.

"Help! Mutiny!"

Oscar the cat had decided to take over Captain Merlin's boat. He had tied up Ernie and Mr Pickles and was feeling very pleased with himself.

"Hey, this is my boat," Captain Merlin barked, "so clear off!"

"Not now it isn't," Oscar purred. "I've taken charge and you're going to have to walk the plank!"

Captain Merlin didn't really want to walk the plank, as he couldn't swim very well. "Oh, I wish I was back home safely in my kennel," he whined.

As soon as he said the magic word, "wish", his collar flashed and sparkled.

Merlin arrived back safely in front of his kennel. Ernie came by carrying a large new plank of wood. "I have to go and mend Miss Parkway's garden fence," he explained. "Do you fancy a walk?"

"Not right now, thank you," Merlin barked. "I think I've had enough of planks and walking for one day!"

Merlin's Quiz

We hope that you have enjoyed reading Merlin's magical annual. Now here is a quiz for you to try. All of the answers are somewhere in the book, but if you are in a hurry you could always look at the bottom of the next page!

1 Where does Merlin live?

2 What colour is Merlin's magical collar?

3 When Merlin wishes he was a secret agent, what is his special secret-agent gadget?

4 One of Merlin's best friends is a hedgehog. What is his name?

5 What special word makes Merlin's magical collar work?

10 Who looks after Merlin?

9 In "Merlin and the Lost Bone", what does Merlin grab from Oscar the cat when he has wished himself invisible?

8 Merlin's best friend is another dog. What is her name?

7 What is Merlin's favourite food?

6 In "Merlin and the Ghost", what do Ernie and Merlin find standing in the hallway of the castle?

Sandybay Harbour

A harbour is a place by the sea where it is safe to leave boats so the tides and bad weather won't damage them.

Ernie, the Harbour Master, keeps his boat, the Salty Sea Dog, at Sandybay Harbour. Whenever he gets the time, he likes to do little jobs on the boat to keep it working well and looking nice and bright.

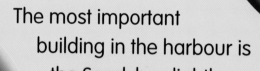

The most important building in the harbour is the Sandybay lighthouse. A lighthouse is a building with a very bright light on top that can be seen from a long way away. The light warns passing ships that they are close to land and should be careful.

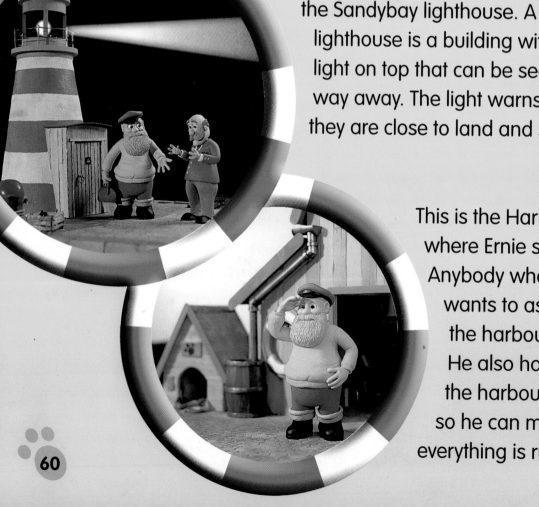

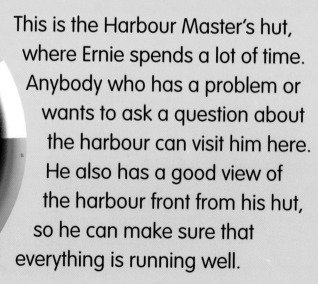

This is the Harbour Master's hut, where Ernie spends a lot of time. Anybody who has a problem or wants to ask a question about the harbour can visit him here. He also has a good view of the harbour front from his hut, so he can make sure that everything is running well.

These cottages were built a long, long time ago and used to belong to the fishermen who worked in Sandybay. Miss Parkway lives in the pink one with Kizzie, and Mr Pickles lives in the blue one next door.

This is the Sandybay Harbour shop. People come here to buy groceries, stamps and postcards. Mr and Mrs Crabtree own the shop and they like to keep fresh fruit and vegetables on a stall outside under a large red and white canopy.

This is the harbour front, where the fishing boats come at the end of the day to unload their fish for the market. Mr Pickles and Mr Crabtree like to come here for some peace and quiet and to do a little fishing of their own.

This is the Sandybay cannon. It is very old and on special occasions, like holidays and anniversaries, Mr Pickles fires it.

Merlin the guide dog puppy

This is a picture of Merlin the Magical Puppy meeting a real-life puppy, also called Merlin, who will grow up to be a guide dog for the blind.